are you ready to be a
HERO?

Written by Dr. Jay Lipoff

Illustrated by Mariko Sakemi

ISBN: 0983614725

ISBN-13: 978-0-9836147-2-2

DEDICATION

The mission of the 501c.3 nonprofit organization, Foundation 4 Heroes, is to inspire children and encourage them to find the superhero inside each of them, whether they are in school or facing adversity in a hospital setting. They are truly the strongest and bravest heroes we know and this book is dedicated to them and their families.

Another important part of our mission is to visit and thank Veterans, Wounded Warriors, and their families, for their courage, their service and their sacrifice.

All of the proceeds from this book will be used so we can continue our mission to be supportive of all heroes.

ACKNOWLEDGEMENTS

Special thanks go to Mike and Laura Batson, Edward Tully and all of the other volunteers that make this organization capable of doing great things. Also thank you to everyone else who has supported our efforts.

Most importantly to my family who has tolerated my absences, the countless hours working on Foundation projects, costumes and accumulation of gifts for children. Without their support and understanding this would not be possible.

It was just a normal day in Matthew's school until his teacher, Mrs. Clark, made a big announcement. She told the class that they would be having a special visitor today. The children became very excited.

Who could it be they all wondered? *"Is it a fireman?"* Carlos asked. *"A policeman?"* shouted Julie. *"An Astronaut?"* responded Reiko. *"Your Mom?"* questioned Eddie. *"The President?"* belted out Lamden.

"*No, no, children. It is a Superhero,*" Mrs. Clark explained. Before anyone could take another guess she told them, "*His name is Captain Foundation.*"

"Captain Foundation represents a small group of everyday people trying to make a difference in people's lives, locally and across the world.

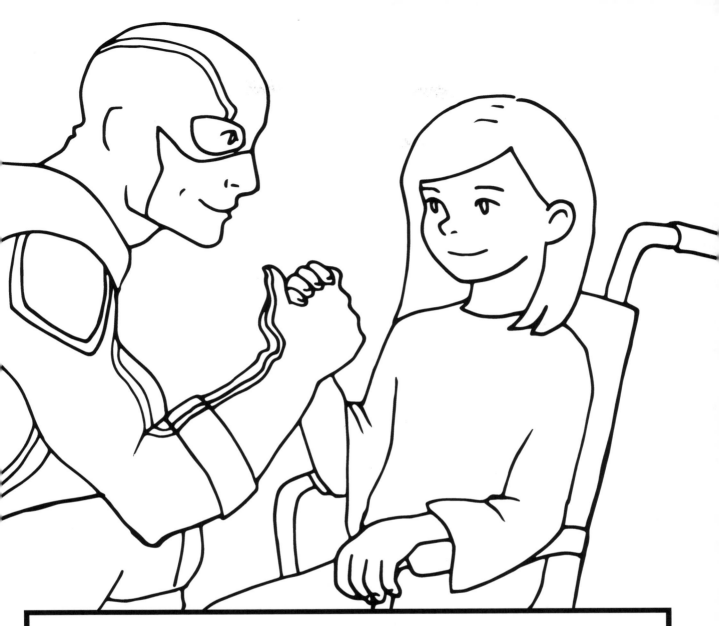

"They help inspire children battling diseases," she told them, "by supporting the families of these children and also teaching all children to, **Be A Hero.** In addition to that, they take time to visit with Wounded Warriors, veterans and their families, to thank these brave men and women for their courage, service to our country to protect our rights and our freedoms, and their sacrifice. They call themselves the Foundation 4 Heroes."

"They may not be able to fly but they can lift your spirits," she said with excitement in her voice. *"They are there to encourage you and teach you all you need to know to **BE A HERO** too,"* she informed them.

The children were excited as many of them had seen members of Foundation 4 Heroes making a difference in their very own communities.

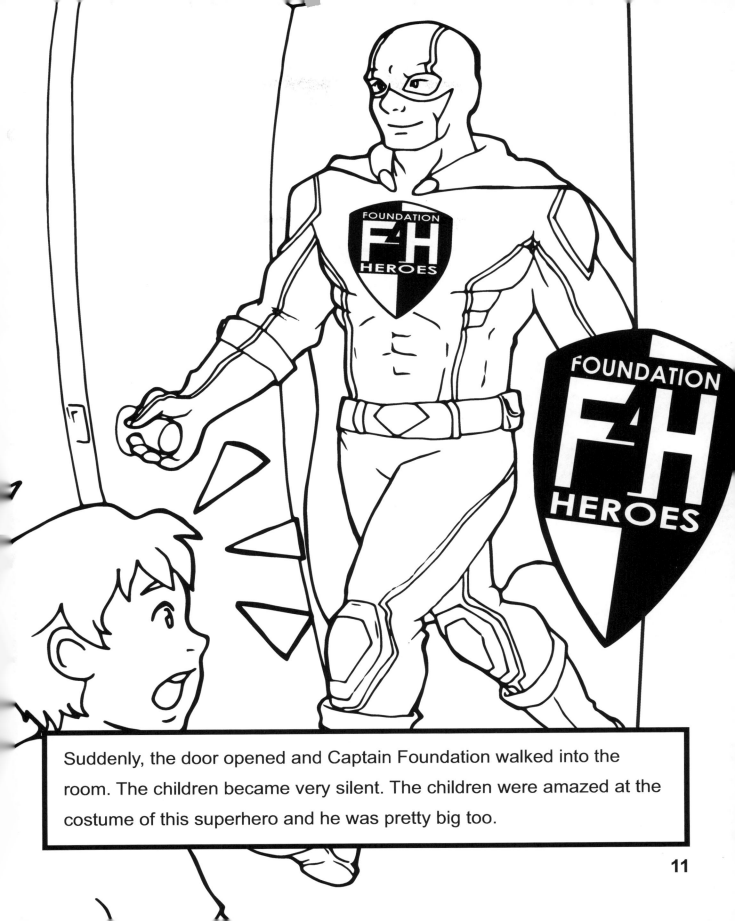

Suddenly, the door opened and Captain Foundation walked into the room. The children became very silent. The children were amazed at the costume of this superhero and he was pretty big too.

5 Simple RULES to be a HERO

Captain Foundation kneeled down, introduced himself and simply asked the children, *"Would you like to be a Superhero?"* Unanimously the children cried out, *"YEEEESSSS!!!"*

*"Okay then. There are 5 simple rules you must learn to **BE A HERO**. You don't need super powers. A hero is someone you can trust. The Police, Firemen, Teachers, Mom and Dad are some heroes you know right now. Every one of you can be a hero right now too! Do you want to **BE A HERO**? Are you ready?"* Again, a loud boom of *"Yes"* echoed into the hallway.

"Superhero School includes 5 steps to becoming a hero," the superhero stated.

"Step #1 is; "Always Do The Right Thing," he said. *"What is it?"* he asked. *"Always Do The Right Thing,"* they said.

Captain Foundation asked, *"If someone leaves trash in the park do you leave it or pick it up and put it in the trash?"* *"Put it in the trash,"* the children shouted. *"Or recycle it,"* added Nickie. *"Yes, way to go!"* said the Caped Captain.

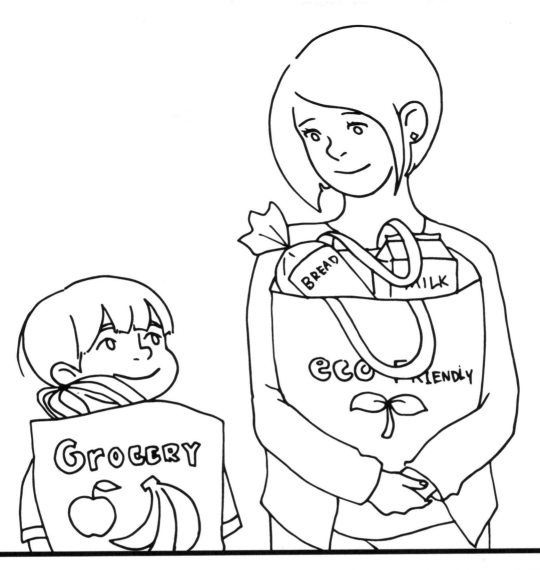

"What if Mom or Dad have groceries in the car? What should you do?" questioned the Foundation 4 Heroes leader. "Help them." "Open the door." "Carry some bags." Responded the heroes in training.

"What if someone says you aren't cool if you don't do something silly or even dangerous to yourself or others; do you just do it to fit in?" the superhero wondered. "No!" the kids cried out.

"Correct. Your friends should always accept you as you are. You have nothing to prove if they are truly a friend," he added.

Step #2 is; "Never Give Up!" he instructed. *"Can you say it for me?"* The children all repeated, *"Never Give Up!"*

"If you are trying to build a bird house and it seems really tough, do you stop?" the superhero questioned. *"No!"* the children shouted.

"When you have some trouble completing a puzzle, do you walk away from it?" he asked the children. *"No!"* the kids stated.

"That means if you are losing in soccer 2 – 1 do you quit?" Captain asked. "No!" the children replied.

"That's right," Captain Foundation explained. "No matter how tough things get, you have to keep trying."

Step #3 is; "Always Listen To Your Parents and Teachers."

"Can you say that with me?" he asked. All at once everyone stated, *"Always Listen To Your Parents and Teachers."*

"Your parents know a lot about life and if you take the time to listen, they will teach you so much. Who listens to their parents when they say it's time for bed?" Cap asked. A couple of hands go up.

18

"Sleep is very important. Not only does your body grow and heal when you rest but if you don't get enough you will do poorly in school, could be cranky and will probably get in trouble," the Hero added.

"Have your folks also warned you about talking to strangers and telling others if someone approaches or touches you? Always say NO and call out for help. Even if someone knows your name, has a lost puppy, offers you candy or a ride somewhere; never go with a stranger."

"Did your parents teach you to look both ways before crossing the road or advise you to ask for help if you aren't sure if something is safe? That's because they are trying to protect you and teach you about important things in life."

"Teachers, policemen, firemen and other authority figures are also super helpful like that so you should listen to them too," finished Captain Foundation.

True	False	Rules About Strangers
		Always stay in a group or with friend
		Avoid a strange vehicle that is stopped
		It is okay to ignore a stranger who knows your name
		Don't follow or ride with a stranger
		Running away from a scary situation is okay
		If you see someone or something unusual, tell an adult immediately
		Screaming loudly is a good defense when in trouble
		Don't accept anything from a stranger even if it is yours
		Never leave from a public place with a stranger
		Always follow your parents' instructions
		When out, travel to the bathroom with friends
		Never tell anyone on the phone or at the door that you are alone

FIRE ESCAPE PLAN!

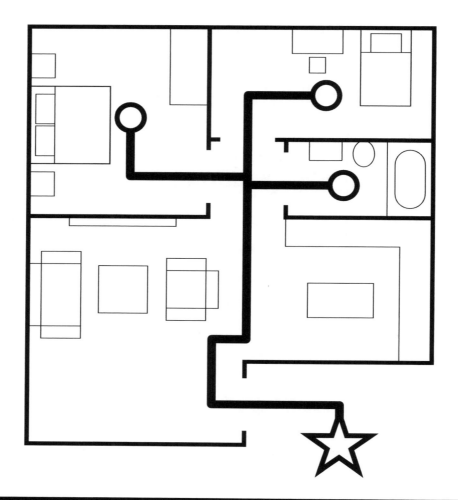

"Do you remember what your parents told you to do if you smell smoke in the house?" Captain asked. A bunch of hands go up. "Let's review some of these rules: call 911 if there's time, don't hide-go outside, call out to other members of the family, never open a hot door, wet a towel or something and cover yourself, stop, drop and roll if your clothing is on fire, stay as low as you can, have an escape plan, have a meeting place and practice exiting quickly." The children nodded their head in agreement.

True	False	Fire Safety Rules
		Make a fire escape plan and choose a meeting place.
		Never hide
		Go outside as quickly as possible
		If you think there's a fire alert others of the danger
		Don't stop to grab items. Get outside.
		Call 911 when possible
		If you see smoke, stay low or crawl
		If you smell smoke cover your face with clothing or a towel
		Stop, drop and roll if your clothes catch fire
		Never open a hot door
		Once outside wait at meeting place

eat healthy

Step #4 is; "Choose Healthy Habits to Keep You Strong." They all repeated, *"Choose Healthy Habits to Keep You Strong."*

"Have you ever heard the saying, you are what you eat?" asked Captain F. *"That's because good nutrition and exercise, are the foundation to every superhero's health,"* he continued.

"Do superheroes play video games all day or do we go outside and kick a ball, ride a bike or play at the park?" he questioned the students. "Play outside and be active," they blurted out.

"When your parents put food on your plate do you eat it without a fuss?" The Captain asked. Then he chuckled as this time the class's response was a little mixed. He informed them, "There are lots of important nutrients and vitamins in foods to make us grow strong and healthy."

SUPERHERO QUIZ:

Circle the foods that are healthy choices.

Apples   Potato   Chips   Soda   Grapes

Vitamins   Water   Cookies   Pizza   Carrots

Broccoli   Fruit Rollup   Pretzels   Soup   Yogurt

Banana   Ice Cream   Fast Food   Candy

Circle the activities that are healthy choices.

Walking   Sleeping   Hours of TV   Playing

Sports   Painting   Brushing Your Teeth   Drawing

Jogging   Stretching   Legos   Telling A Lie   Listening

Reading   Helping   Camping

Circle the traits of a hero and items of a superhero costume.

Strong   Honest   Mask   Power Ring   Lazy   Kind

Sloppy   Boots   Courageous   Super Powers   Helpful

Can Fly   Cap   Utility Belt   Cool Car   Shield

Helmet   Muscles   Gloves

"*The last step to complete your training on how to **Be A Hero is Step #5, Never Be A Bully,***" professed the superhero before them. "*What is it?*" he asked. "*Never Be A Bully,*" replied the children.

"*Have you ever been on the bus, the playground or in the hallway and another kid is teasing and picking on someone else, or someone calls you small or a name? How does that make you feel?*" asked the heroic Captain. One answer was sad, another was angry and then hurt.

The room had quieted down from the earlier excitement. "*That's right. It doesn't make us feel good,*" agreed the Captain. "*You should always be kind to others and treat people as nicely as you want to be treated.*"

The Hero tells the children a personal story. *"My son came home very sad from school one day. I asked him what was wrong. He said he was picked on because he has long hair. I asked him how he felt and he said upset. I explained to him sometimes kids say things to look cool or be tough and get attention. In reality, no one is better than anyone else. There is nothing cool about hurting another person's feelings or injuring them physically."*

"Would you believe the very child that was unkind to my son came to him the next day to apologize and now they are friends. Don't forget that saying you are sorry is very important if you have made a mistake or hurt someone," explained the superhero. The children all smiled and nodded.

"The next time you kids see that someone is being bullied on the bus, the playground or in the hallway, I want you to let a parent or teacher know immediately. Always speak up against anyone who is a bully. Kids you should avoid the bully, ignore them, tell them to stop or stay with your friends. The bottom line is you are not at fault, you are not alone and people care about you and will help resolve this. Every person is different but that doesn't mean they can't be your friend."

That is what it means to *"Be A Hero."*

> *"So everyone let's go through our rules again,"* stated Captain Foundation. *"Are you ready?"*

Step 1: Always Do The Right Thing

Step 2: Never Give Up

Step 3: Always Listen To Your Parents

Step 4: Choose Healthy Habits to Keep You Strong

Step 5: Never Be A Bully

"Congratulations kids! You have officially passed Superhero School," proudly announced Captain Foundation. "You have learned to *"Be A Hero,"* he added.

Matthew reached his hand out to the Foundation 4 Heroes' Superhero and quietly said, *"Thank you Captain Foundation."*

"You are most welcome. Being a hero and providing support to people who need it is what we are all about," said Captain Foundation.

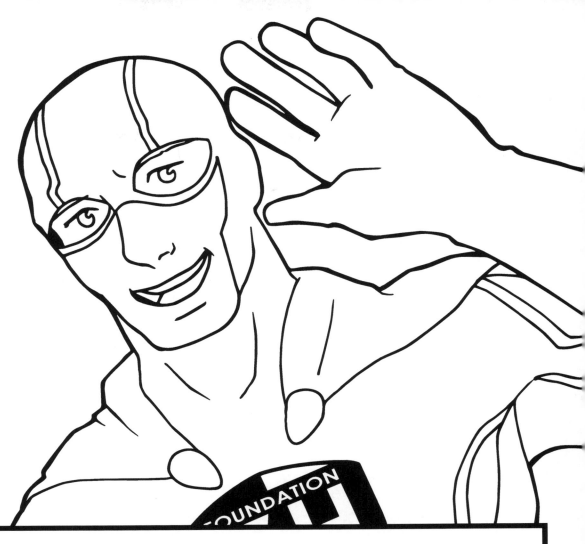

Captain told the children he had to go because he was needed at Children's Hospital to inspire some boys and girls that weren't feeling well. He informed them they could keep an eye on the Foundation 4 Heroes, with their parents' permission, at *www.F4Heroes.com* and on Facebook.

He hugged all of the children and challenged them to draw a picture of what their Superhero costume will look like now that they had learned to *Be A Hero.* He told them to keep thinking of ways they could make a difference in their community by being a Hero to others.

When the day ended, Matthew couldn't wait to tell his parents about all of the cool things he had learned at school that day. Especially that anyone could *BE A HERO.*

The End

AUTHOR BIOGRAPHY

Dr. Jay M. Lipoff visited his first hospital in 1988 with friends while attending Syracuse University. They all dressed as very popular professional wrestlers, and that's how this idea all began.

He received his Bachelor of Science degree from Syracuse University in 1990, a Doctorate of Chiropractic (D.C.) from New York Chiropractic College (NYCC) in 1994 and he became a Certified Fitness Trainer (CFT) in 2005.

He is the owner of Back At Your Best Chiropractic & Physical Therapy, LLC, which is located in Maryland. Dr. Lipoff is also the author of "Back At Your Best: Balancing the Demands of Life With the Needs of Your Body," which is available in book and Kindle format on Amazon.com.

Dr. Lipoff is an Executive Board Member, International Chiropractic Association Council on Fitness and Sports Health Science; had a radio segment, Back At Your Best in 5 Minutes or Less; President and Founder, Foundation 4 Heroes; Co-Founder, Drug Free Training USA; Member, NY Strength-promoting the importance of physical conditioning; has spoken on nationally broadcasted radio interviews, has articles in print and referenced in over 200 print papers, magazines and on websites.

For more information on Foundation 4 Heroes visit them on Facebook at **F4Heroes**, **www.f4heroes.com** or call **844-F4Heroes**.

THE MAKING OF A HERO

Decades ago Ray and Sallie Hero took a family trip to Yellowstone National Park with their son Hart. He was named for his grandfather who served as a Captain in the United States Military. They named him Hart because it meant brave and strong and they wanted him to be just that when he grew older.

While exploring the park they observed some animals, Old Faithful the geyser, went hiking in the woods and that's when they became separated and the young boy was on his own. Despite hours of searching and calling out; Hart was never found.

He felt alone and scared, like anyone would, when facing such a dramatic situation. After conquering his initial fears, he knew he could make it and he remembered what his parents had taught him growing up. His survival skills and instincts took over. He knew he needed water, shelter and food. If he could get that he would be okay.

Many weeks passed and Hart had built a wonderful lean-to, learned to make a net to catch fish and discovered which leaves and berries were edible. He still wondered how much longer before he could finally be home? Thunderstorms were rolling in and he was worried because they seemed to be endless.

Weeks later Hart was found by a man named Dan who was walking his dog along the trails. Hart had been wandering through the forest, hungry and weakened for what could have been days or weeks.

Dan was a Wounded Warrior who had proudly served in the United States Marine Corps. He decided to take him under his wing. Due to Hart's surviving in the wilderness for such a long time he had grown very sick from insect bites, famine and had sustained multiple injuries from falls. Dan patched him up a bit and then brought him to a local hospital for much needed treatment.

Hart was taken to several hospitals due to complications of his sickness, age and health. While recovering over the next few months, Hart really grew an appreciation for the care he was receiving and the hard-working healthcare professionals that looked after him and the other children. They were great.

As he grew stronger he exercised and trained with Dan and learned many things; to always do the right thing, never give up, listen to your parents, make healthy choices and never be a bully to others.

While Hart was in school he continued to eat well, train to be an elite athlete and competitor in sports. Hart became bigger and more muscular and started to even resemble a superhero's stature.

Years went by and upon his college graduation Hart received a message that his parents had been located and were anxious to see him. It was wonderful to see his parents after all this time. So when the ceremonies ended Hart decided to tell everyone his plans for the future.

He wanted to find a way to help other children dealing with pain and an uncertain future, like he experienced when he was ill. Hart was determined and steadfast to create some type of foundation of inspiration, hope and support to make a difference in their lives.

These children are so strong and brave facing illness and disease like they do. They were definitely true heroes in his mind and that included the family members surrounding them.

Hart also learned to respect Veterans, like Dan the Wounded Warrior, who had served and are bravely serving our country today. They all have shown tremendous courage and made sacrifices that he would not take for granted. He would find a way to show them his appreciation as well.

That's why Hart Hero founded the Foundation 4 Heroes. Today he visits children in schools, inspires children in hospitals and thanks and shows support for Veterans. He is known to the community as a hero named Captain Foundation.

On these next few pages, draw a picture of what you would look like if you were a superhero and tell me what your super powers are.

What Is Your Superhero Name?

_____

What Superhero Items Do You Have? (list as many as you need):

Cape
_____   _____

_____   _____

_____   _____

_____   _____

What Are Your Superpowers?

Can Fly
_____   _____

_____   _____

_____   _____

_____   _____

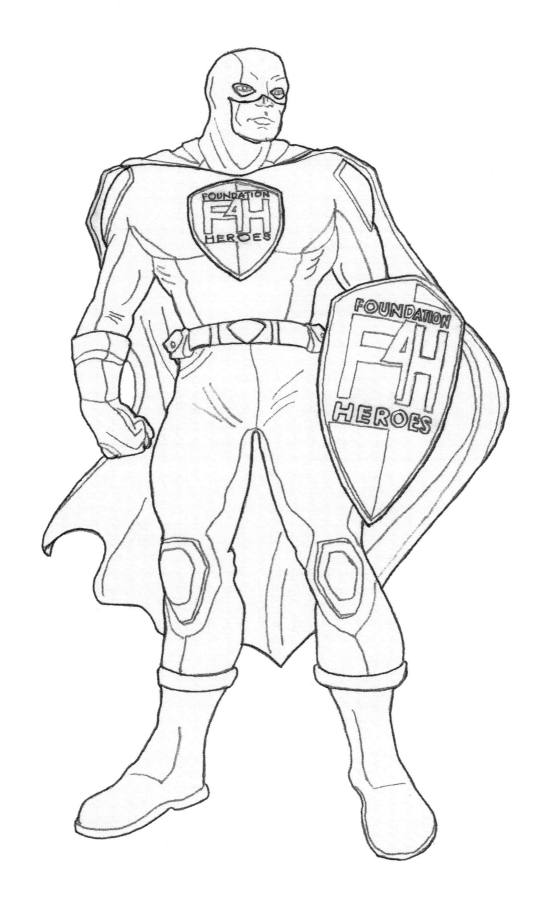

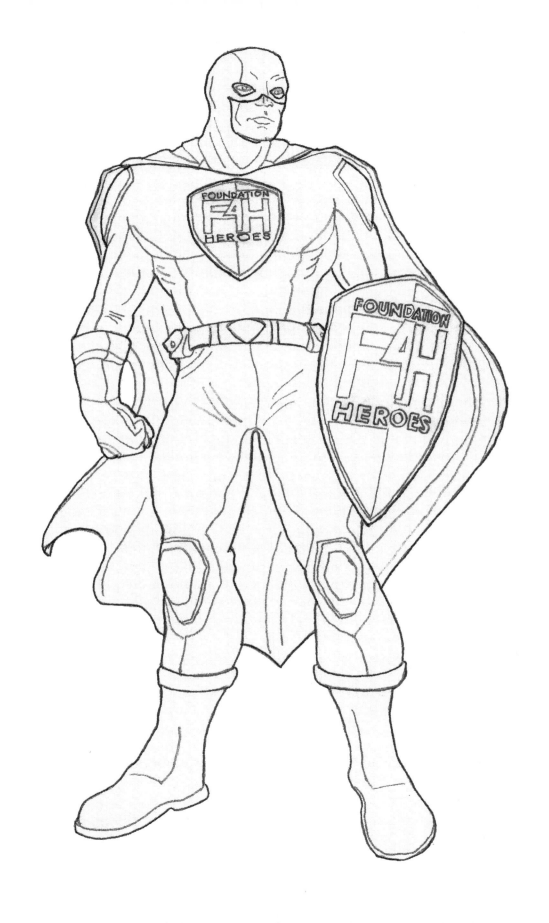

Made in the USA
San Bernardino, CA
21 May 2017